The Dragon

Tree

Wendy Guilfoyle

DEDICATION

"To believe in the things you can see is no belief at all. To believe in the unseen is a triumph and a blessing". Lincoln

... to all those who still believe in the unseen.

CONTENTS

Acknowledgments

ACKNOWLEDGMENTS

My thanks go to Maggie Bennet for help with the early editing, to Shoo Raynor and Mark Crilley for their video tutorials, and to my friends Kay, Julia and Penny for patiently listening to my writing triumphs and despairs over many months. Also, to my sister, Mary Jones, who supports me in all my endeavours. Mostly, my thanks go to friends Paul, Lee and Ian for their support, encouragement and critiques. Without them the book may not have been finished.

1 THE DAY IT ALL WENT TERRIBLY WRONG

It was a day of celebration. Everyone was excited. The village green was full of large tables laden with great joints of roast meats and vegetables, soups and stews, delicious cakes and sweets. There were flagons of beer and mead. Brightly coloured flags and bunting danced in the breeze. People bustled about, children ran around getting in the way, dragons hooted and whistled, jostling for position to be first in line for the big clean up.

The Guild of Washers marched about importantly, carrying bowls of sweet smelling, herbal oils and special detergents to clean the dragons' scales and wings.

The festivities and cleaning began with loud music and cheers. The villagers were busy tucking into pies and chicken legs and roast beef sandwiches. Children darted about trying to get a big piece of cake before they were made to eat the vegetables and playing hide and seek with their young dragon friends. The dragons that had been washed and oiled were now clean and shining. They stretched and flexed their supple wings, delighted with their comfortable skin and glistening appearance. Everyone was relaxed and having a wonderful time on this special day.

Suddenly, alarm calls went up from all around the village. Startled and frightened, the people and dragons looked around to see what the danger was. Was it a pack of wolves, bears or a family of wild boar digging up their winter crops? No! A vast dark cloud was streaming towards them at great speed, swirling and roiling like a great thunderstorm, but much, much worse. Then they saw what it was. This was no storm but a horde of marauding, wild dragons. Wyverns! They were large, brutish creatures, dirty, dark, drab and murderous. Before anyone could flee for safety or any defence arranged, the Wyverns swooped down on the festivities, turning over tables, eating or trampling on the food, slaying men, women and children alike. It was terrifying. The battle was soon over. Many beautiful dragons and people were killed that day. All surviving dragons were rounded up and taken prisoner to be used as slaves.

2 A QUICK RECAP IN WHICH WE GO BACK SEVEN YEARS

As you have guessed this was no ordinary village. Many generations ago, a tribe of beautiful dragons had appeared and befriended the people. These were not the wild fire-breathing dragons that had just wreaked devastation on their homes. Nor were they the small heraldic, treble-singing dragons of Wales; nor the swirling, elemental dragons of China that writhe or slumber in the earth, the air, the water and in the clouds.

No. These were the most beautiful and gentle dragons you could ever imagine. If I said they were emerald or scarlet or ultra-marine that would only be half true. They were iridescent; their scales sparkled and shimmered like shot-silk or like the shifting rainbow colours you see when sunlight shines on oily puddles. Also, they could speak in the people's own language and understand when they were spoken to.

Very quickly the dragons and the people developed a lifestyle of mutual friendship and help. The dragons helped by carrying the people here and there to visit family, to take them and their animals to market. The bigger ones could even pull ploughs so the farmers could plant corn and vegetables to produce food for everyone. With the dragons help, they had marvelously bountiful harvests.

In return the people fed them with some of their cattle and sheep and built large shelters to keep them warm and dry. Of course, they also promised to take care of their wings and scales, horns and claws with special oils and herbal cleansers. Hence the Washing Day which had developed into a wonderful day of feasting and celebration.

There is one more thing for you to know, to make sense of the rest of the story.

Seven years previously a special event had occurred. Arianrod, a golden-red dragon had laid an egg and it was soon to hatch out, probably on Washing Day. The whole village was tense with excitement, anticipating a beautiful, sturdy, little hatchling in the most glorious of colours. However, when the egg finally cracked open, a tiny dragon struggled out on thin wobbly legs. Everyone gasped. Not only was the dragon *very* small, not at all usual for baby dragons, it was pearly white! No dragon before or since had hatched white. No one knew what to say. Was it a good thing? Would he develop a colour as he grew older? Would he grow older? After all, he was *very small*.

He did survive, but remained pearly white and small. His wings grew, but were neither big nor strong like those of the other young dragons. Aedelwine [for they named him 'noble friend'] couldn't keep up with their games or with the tasks they were set to do. The other dragons teased and taunted him constantly, pushing him about and calling him names.

They eventually got tired of this sport because he never retaliated, so they just ignored him all together. That was almost worse. Even though he was relieved to be spared the bullying, he felt left out, very lonely and useless.

To comfort himself, Aedelwine would get up very early

and walk quietly down to the big river that flowed near the village. It was very close to where the river merged with the sea, so it was very wide, and the levels rose and fell with the ocean tides. He loved it there. It was so peaceful. He began to sing to himself and discovered he had the most beautiful singing voice, unlike all the other dragons. He sang about his sadness and loneliness, his joys and his appreciation of the natural beauty he saw all around him.

Every morning he would sit on a tree stump and sing to the rising sun until it was high in the sky. The singing soothed his sadness and he forgot about being small and weak. His singing was so melodious that the spirits of the river, the Naiads, and the spirits of the trees and forests, the Dryads, began to gather there every dawn to listen to him. He loved that more than anything, to know that they enjoyed his singing. They became friends and companions and he stopped feeling so lonely. The nature spirits would share their worries and problems with Aedelwine. He would listen very carefully and always found something to say that was encouraging or made sense of their situation.

Now and then some of the villagers would come to listen to his singing for a break from their hard-working day. This made him very happy; feel more a part of the village and less isolated. Two villagers soon came to visit him every day - two children, a brother and a sister. Aedelwine's heart glowed with love and happiness when they were there. They became good friends very quickly. In this manner the years passed. The pearly dragon grew a bit more and learned to fly, but only short distances and low to the ground as he needed to stop and rest every now and then.

3
AEDELWINE'S SEVENTH BIRTHDAY

Like all the dragons, Aedelwine loved "Washing Day". Today was even more special, as it was his Seventh Birthday, a very special dragon birthday! The very special thing that even the people didn't know about was that when they became seven, dragons were able to talk to each other over long distances just with their thoughts. We call it telepathy nowadays, but for them it was just what they did. How otherwise could they arrange their wide-ranging lives? Someone would need to know when to expect them home for tea and there were no mobile phones then.

As usual the village was decked out with flags and ribbons. The long tables were brought out onto the green and were soon laden with every kind of the most wonderful food for the people and special dishes for the dragons.

The dragons crowded round the Guild of Washers, jostling to be first in line, asking them to hurry up. When they all talked together it was like an orchestra playing as each dragon had a tone of voice which went with their particular colour. The red dragons had warm, rich voices, blue dragons had rippling voices like a stream, yellow dragons had more metallic, bell-like tones. Sadly, none of them could sing. If they tried, it came out all squeaky and wrong. No other dragon but Aedelwine had a beautiful singing voice.

The festivities were well on their way when the alarm calls went out and those terrible dragons swept into the village and (as we saw at the beginning), many people and dragons were killed. The surviving dragons were rounded up and held prisoners.

The largest of these vicious dragons, their leader Eadwig (meaning wealth gained from war), plucked the Master

Washer up into the air in his sabre-sharp claws. With a
harsh, grating voice like rusty metal scraping on metal,
mean and cruel, the kind of voice that sent icicles of terror
rushing through you, he said,

"You will come with us and tend us as you tend these
creatures here". He nodded disdainfully in the direction of
the imprisoned and injured. "If you don't, we will just
destroy your village and all the humans who live here". To
emphasise his threat, he turned his head and casually blew
a jet of flame at a nearby cottage. Such was the intense
heat and force of the flame that the cottage, everything
and anybody inside were a smoking heap of ash in an
instant. The villagers huddled together, petrified by such a
show of power and destruction.

"If you come now, we will leave with the prisoners, some
sheep and cattle and let the people live"

The Master knew he had no choice but to go with them, as
they demanded.

"A good decision," continued Eadwig. "However, to
ensure the future safety of your village, we demand a tithe.
Each year, we will return for a number of your cattle and
sheep. You will tether them up there". He indicated a
higher rocky place some distance away. "We will have an
annual feast like you".

He smiled a cruel and triumphant smile as gasps and cries
of horror rose from the terrified villagers.

"As I said, if you don't …" He shrugged and sent a second jet of flame reducing a second cottage and all its contents to ashes in moments.

The people had to agree and so for a few years they made their payment of precious cattle and sheep. It hurt them deeply for they cared for their animals; all of them were named and known to them.

4
A CHANGE IN THE AGREEMENT

As time went by, in their greed, the Wyverns took more cattle than could be replaced and soon there were only a very few left. The villagers needed some animals for their own food, wool from the sheep for clothes, leather to make shoes, as well as to breed more cattle and sheep to feed the dragons. The day came when they couldn't leave any more animals up on the rocks above the village till more calves and lambs had been born.

Eadwig thundered into the village.

"What is the meaning of this? Why no animals? Are you going back on your agreement?"

"We have very few left, "explained the Mayor. We need to keep what are left to breed more for you to have. If you have all of these there will be no more. Ever!"

The Wyvern thought for a moment. The animals had been a big part of their yearly feast. All his tribe had got used to these festivities. They would challenge his leadership if it stopped now. He needed a different ransom to keep the village under his control, but he understood that he needed to allow the numbers of the animals to build up again.

"No matter," he said. "We will take a smaller tithe until such time as your herds have recovered. Instead of the cattle, you will leave two of your children tethered in that same place; if you don't, we will destroy your village".

Once again, there came a burst of flame from Eadwig's mouth and another cottage exploded in flames, reduced to rubble and ash in the blink of an eye. Numb with fear the people agreed. Not waiting any longer, Eadwig seized two children nearest to him, laughed and flew away, the screams of the children filling the air until they were carried away over the hills.

Their Mother ran after them, screaming and crying. She had to be restrained and brought gently back. She had other children who needed her now more than ever. The horror of what they had been forced to agree to do fell around them in a heavy shroud of grief and helplessness. What defence did they have against these Wyverns? They were so huge and callous; so powerful. If the people resisted, they would all be burned to ashes. Without all their lovely dragon friends and knowing that each year two more children would have to be sacrificed, life became a struggle, greyer, increasingly sad and filled with anguish.

Every year, the herbalists of the ransomed village tried all manner of herbs, tree barks and seeds from ancient recipes found in their archives, in order to sedate the children to lessen the terror of their ordeal. They helped a bit but were never strong enough. Everyone was starving anyway. They were not able to eat the animals because they wanted their herds and flocks to increase as quickly as possible so they could use these as the ransom again and spare their children. Without their dragons they were not so successful at hunting the wild animals, nor were they able to prepare the ground properly. Many of the seeds failed to germinate and those that did, grew small. Yields got worse each year. Times were desperate.

5 DESPERATE TIMES; DESPERATE DECISIONS

Times were desperate for the captive dragons as well. As slaves to those savage and wild Wyverns, they were worked to exhaustion, beaten and half starved. If they failed to work as their captors directed them, or if they tried to escape, they were beaten, tortured and eventually killed. It was especially hard for Aedelwine. He was taunted and spat on for being small and weak. He was deliberately given tasks too heavy for him or made to fly too far, and then they would beat him and kick him for taking too long. The only thing that kept him and the other dragons going was their love for each other, their kind hearts and compassion which they conveyed to each other through their thoughts. The Wyverns did not have this special skill so were not aware of this.

Every year, the evil Wyverns chose one of their own young male dragons to collect and kill the children from the village, kill them and carry their bodies back to their settlement. It was a test for young Wyverns to become a warrior of their tribe and not usually something entrusted to slaves.

The time came around again to send a young dragon to collect the children from the post amongst the rocks. Eadwig saw how he could have some fun and torment this small weak dragon even more severely.

"You! Weakling! You will be the one to be tested for initiation this year. If you don't return with the tithe (meaning the two children) we will kill your mother, father and brother" – he paused and smiled his terrible smile – "eventually, after we have burned the village to the ground and seized all the villagers".

Aedelwine looked up at his mother, father and brother whom he loved and honoured dearly. He could not bear to think of them being tortured. Sadly, he left to travel to that frightful place in the rocks. Slowly and with a heavy heart he walked up the now well-worn track to the place where the children would be tied. The path was so arranged that the post was not visible until he was very close. He knew he couldn't kill them, but if he didn't the whole village would be destroyed and his family tortured and killed. Slowly, slowly he wound his way up the track, thinking of his dear Mother and Father. He rounded the last bend. He saw the terrified children, tethered to the post like cattle, clinging to each other, their eyes shut tight.

Aedelwine was horrified. He recognised them. They were his two special friends who used to come to listen to him sing to the rising sun each morning along with the Naiads and Dryads! His heart ached as he remembered the warm sun, the sound of the river as it told of all the things it had seen on its journey from the mountains far away, the bird song and the smell of the wild flowers and the fresh grass that grew there.

The children's whimpers jerked him back to the present and the task ahead of him. Something snapped inside him. He knew in an instant what he would have to do and with the knowing came the strength and courage to carry out the plan. He saw his Mother in his inner eye; would she understand? He marched with determination towards the cowering children…

Bending his head close to the children till they could feel his breath on their heads…

"Hush!" he whispered. "Don't be frightened. It is I, Aedelwine. Keep still! I am going to break your bonds. Now climb on me. We are going to stop this fearful thing and we will save the villagers".

The children could hardly believe their ears. It was their best friend, still alive. They threw their arms around his neck, laughing and crying with joy and relief.

Aedelwine spoke urgently to them. "Climb up and hold tight. Quickly! We will celebrate when it is all over".

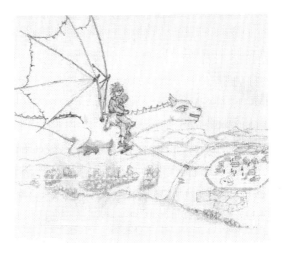

Overjoyed the children scrambled onto his back and to their amazement they took off into the air and sped down to the village. The villagers had been anxiously waiting and listening for the inevitable screams, worried by the silence, and then they saw their very own Aedelwine flying at speed towards them with the two children, very much alive, on his back.

6 THE EVACUATION

He cut their welcome and rejoicing short. "Hurry! Gather only the things you cannot manage without, like a few clothes and cooking pots. Hide what animals you have left deep in the wood out of sight, together with a few other belongings that may be too heavy to carry now in haste. I will carry you over the river where you can hide in the dense forest that grows there. We have to be quick to get you all out before the Wyverns arrive. When I don't return, they will fly here to destroy everything".
The people needed no more prompting. They rushed about gathering family, clothes, blankets and chickens. Sheep and cattle were herded out of sight and penned in.

Aedelwine set off with a heavy load and was quickly over the river. He showed the villagers where to go, then went back for the next group. Several trips would be needed, so speed was essential if the job was to be finished in time.

Things began to look more hopeful.

Meanwhile back at the wild dragons' settlement, Eadwig waited impatiently for the return of the dragon with the ransom. He knew how long the journey should take. He even made allowances for the fact that the weak young slave would be slower than one of his fine, healthy youngsters.

"Still", Eadwig thought," the slave should surely have arrived by now".

The rest of the tribe were getting restless, eager to start on their annual feast. Soon, he knew, they would get angry and rebel against him.

Roaring in anger and frustration, Eadwig gathered his tribe together. Leaving only a few of the older wyverns behind to guard the weak prisoners, (with the promise that they would return with some of the "feast" for them), they all set off for the village. They were relishing the thought of the sport to come, burning the houses and catching and killing the people as they fled. They would have their feast day after all.

They were terrible indeed.

Back at the village, Aedelwine had one last trip to make. It was the biggest and heaviest load because he knew the Wyverns would soon be there and he wanted to make sure everyone would be rescued. There wasn't much time.

When he saw the first of the wild dragons appear in the distance, fear and desperation lifted him off the ground, even though he was very weary. He headed straight for the river. He was very near, but very tired and his initial burst of strength was fading. He was getting slower and slower and closer to the ground. Everyone urged him to keep going, cheering and making themselves as light as they could, even throwing their goods overboard to lighten his load. They were now above the river and the danger was even greater. He was so close to the water; he would soon be in the river. He would die instantly and all his precious cargo would be swept out to sea. Try as he might he could not lift his wings enough to keep them airborne. The villagers on the shore were shouting, grabbing sticks, anything to help get survivors out... Just as he was about to hit the water, a massive wave surged upstream, carrying with it a huge raft of trees, branches and reeds. It swept under the dragon catching him neatly just in time, holding him high above the water. The raft, dragon and people were carried safely over to the distant bank of the river and deposited gently right at the edge of the forest.

Thankful for their magical, last minute rescue and

deliverance, the villagers hastily gathered children and goods and scrambled into the shelter of the trees before the wild dragons could see where they were hiding.

The Naiads had been watching the rescue mission, overjoyed at the return of their beloved, much missed dragon. Seeing that their dear friend was in grave and mortal danger, they had caused a wave to race up-river gathering debris, trees and branches, creating a raft big enough to catch the dragon and his cargo and carry them to safety.

The Dryads had also been watching the drama unfold and praised the Naiads for their quick thinking in creating the raft. However, there was a new danger of the people being discovered before they could completely hide themselves from sight. Using all their skills, The Wood Sprites began weaving trees together, twisting branches to form dense canopies, causing new trees to shoot up quickly, creating new thickets around the people who were too overcome to move quickly to the shelter of the forest. It was all so very urgent. Hope of a new life for the whole village hung in the balance. Would Aedelwine's valiant efforts succeed or had they all been in vain?

7 A MIRACLE AND A REUNION

The savage dragons were close by. The villagers could hear their roars. Enraged at finding the village deserted, robbed of their sport and feast, they flamed everything in sight, then flew around searching for the white dragon who had tricked them and for the villagers whom they knew had to be somewhere close by. Eventually they saw Aedelwine on his last trip across the river and saw how close he was to the water. The Wyverns planned to swoop down on him, pushing him into the water, killing him instantly with all the men, women and children he was carrying…

Flying swiftly, they were almost upon the fleeing group, when a vast wall of water, a tsunami, thirty feet high engulfed them all in seconds, killing them instantly.

The Naiads, for it was them who had created this wall of water, washed them all back upstream across the river to the village they had destroyed and beyond. They made the water quickly recede, dumping their large bodies randomly along the valley floor.

Back at the Wyverns' settlement the imprisoned dragons were not as weak as Eadwig had supposed. They loved Aedelwine and were outraged that he had been sent on such a mission. They determined to go to his rescue. They had had enough of the cruelty of the Wyverns and thought it better to die in the attempt to escape, than go on forever as they had been.

As you know, they had quickly realised that the wild dragons did not have their gift of telepathy so had always used this silent way of communicating throughout their captivity. Using their thoughts, they quickly agreed what they would do. They couldn't risk telling the Master Washer their plans. The poor man was almost out of his mind with fear and hunger from his long imprisonment and the excessive demands made on him by Eadwig. He was in no state to agree or otherwise.

The stronger captives overpowered and killed the guards. One of then seized the Master and they all flew to the aid of their young dragon. How did they know where to go? By sending hasty pictures of his plan, telepathically,

Aedelwine had been able to show his Mother and Father what he planned to do when he came to his momentous and courageous decision back amongst the rocks. They flew to the village first and were alarmed to see that it was deserted and in ruins. What had happened here? They followed the Wyverns' trail of burned trees and scorched fields that led towards the river, fearful of what they would find.

What they found were the bodies of the drowned, wild dragons piled and scattered along the valley floor. Then they heard cheering and singing from the other side of the river. The villagers, seeing the destruction of their tormentors, were celebrating the courage and newfound strength of their valiant little rescuer.

Then they saw all their own lovely, kind dragons fly into view across the river.

They were overjoyed. There was such rejoicing as they ran here and there welcoming them, hugging them, exclaiming at their dull and dirty scales and wings.

Then they noticed Aedelwine and stopped singing. They realised that he was lying unmoving, exhausted, overcome by the terror, determination and sheer physical effort of his miraculous rescue mission.

They approached quietly, warily; afraid his great effort had killed him. Arianrod came close to him. "Aedelwine! Aedelwine! Wake up. It is your mother speaking".

Aedelwine thought he must be dreaming that he could hear her voice. He thought all the dragons were still back in the Wyvern settlement. He was not sure if he had been successful in sending his family his hasty message, or if they had received it.

He opened his eyes slowly. No! he wasn't dreaming. There was his Mother, his Father, brother and all the colourful dragons, together with the Master Washer, who was still bewildered and muddled, but sensed that they were all free at last.

When they were all reunited, they lamented the dragons and children who had been killed and the loss of their homes back in the village. They shared their stories of their experiences during the reign of terror and imprisonment, but they were alive and had a new future.

Soon necessity cut through the stories and the tears as the sun was setting lower in the sky and it would be dark in no time. They created a clearing amongst the trees then worn out by the excitement and anxiety of the events of the day, they all fell asleep on the leaves in a circle, tucked up close to their dear friends the dragons. Quietly, the Dryads made a fence of dense bushes and trees all around them to keep out the wild animals.

8 A NEW START

The next day they all set to work to make a temporary camp in the shelter of the forest, to fetch their few cattle and sheep, that were waiting patiently near their old village, and sort out the hens. The Washing Master, now getting his wits and his energy back, worked with his old colleagues to make new shampoos and gathered special oils to clean the dragons. They were very crusty and dirty after their captivity. No festivities this time. It was urgent work and a wonderful way of welcoming their friends back home. The dragons were very relieved to have clean and flexible wings and smooth scales again.

With the help of the dragons, the people soon built a new village amongst the trees at the top of the hill. They caught deer and wild boar to eat until their herds and flocks had recovered in number. Later they created fields, planted crops and fruit trees. The Dryads taught them to work with the gnomes of the earth and the spirits of the plants, learning what the soil and plants needed to thrive. Their yields were excellent and the food nutritious. The people and the dragons flourished – all except Aedelwine. He never fully recovered from his ordeal as a prisoner and the heroic rescue of a whole village. The people understood. It would take everyone a long time to recover fully from all that had happened during those dreadful years. They made special herbal teas to speed his recovery and built a shelter for him, and others, where they could be quiet when they needed.

He was sorry he was not able to help with the rebuilding and fieldwork. His old feelings of being small, weak and useless returned, though no-one bullied or teased him. The people could see that he was very sad and Arianrod spent a lot of time with him. She was so proud of him and how he had saved the village and enabled her and the other dragons to escape. She listened carefully as he told her about the events, how afraid but determined he had felt when he decided on his audacious plan; how anxious and fearful he felt when his strength waned and it seemed they would end up in the river. She heard all that he said and really understood why he was now so exhausted and overcome. Aedelwine felt better for telling her all that he had felt and for the understanding she had of his situation. He told her how badly he felt now that everything was over and that he was still unable to help with the tasks the other dragons were able to do.

Arianrod asked him if there was anything, no matter how small, he felt he could do; something he enjoyed doing. Without hesitation he said he loved to sing but was worried that it would not be that important, when there was so much to do, rebuilding everything. His Mother thought for a while, then asked him what kind of songs did he know. Were they only the sad, slow songs he had sung over the last few days or did he know cheerful, upbeat songs as well?

"Oh yes!" he replied. "I know lots!"

"Then that shall be your job, to sing to the people and the dragons to soothe our grief, to encourage us as we work, to remind us of how beautiful life is and to sing us to sleep in the evening as we sit around our fires".

Families, who had had children taken by the dragons in the bad days, came to visit him. They shared their deep grief and loss with him. He listened carefully and understood how they felt. The telling of their sorrows and knowing they were understood helped heal their pain.

He was never expected to do any heavy work so in the morning he sat on the river bank and sang songs of thanks, joy and wonder to the Dryads who had hidden his people with trees and to the Naiads who had saved him and destroyed the terrible dragons with the waves. The sprites gathered around him, overjoyed to hear his beautiful voice once again. Then he would walk to the fields and the new village and sing cheerful songs, giving people renewed energy as they worked. In the evening everyone would gather round the fire to listen to his lullabies. Doing what he loved in this way, he felt more a part of the village than he had ever done before. He was very happy.

The two children whom he had saved that momentous day came to see him almost every day. They came to sing, to reminisce and chat about this and that as friends do.

9 TIMES CHANGE

Years passed and ever more years. Soon it was their children, then their grandchildren and their great, great-grandchildren who came to sit with him and chat. Generations of people came and went. The people gradually forgot how they had been saved by a little pearly dragon and about the dragons with whom they lived in harmony. People were busy with new machinery, building houses and roads, building huge factories.

The dragons were neglected and eventually became almost forgotten. They became the subject of myths and legends. It was no longer safe to be seen. They would be hunted or captured and put in a zoo and "investigated", which sounded worse than captivity.

It was time for them to leave for another, safer place. The dragons, who lived many long years, felt no anger towards the humans. It had always been the same. They stayed as long as they were needed and loved, then moved on to the next place where they could help. Arianrod asked

Aedelwine if he would come with them to find a new, safer home.

"No, I don't think so," he said. "I will stay here with the people, the Naiads and Dryads; they are my family too and I am not strong enough for another adventure or a long journey. We can always talk to each other, as we have in the past."

Arianrod's heart was full of sadness. She loved Aedelwine dearly and would miss his songs and his calm and understanding presence. She also understood that he would not be strong enough to make the journey they would be undertaking. With heavy hearts, she and the other dragons said goodbye. Aedelwine sang their favourite songs and songs of farewell as they drifted away west, into the sunset.

The sprites couldn't allow him to be seen by the people or hurt by their cars and lorries, so they disguised him as a tall, strong tree that would stay alive and green for many long years. He would be safe from human eyes but would still be able to sing to the rising sun and they could continue to come each day to listen in delight.

However, if you have the eyes to see and you look carefully as you leave the big Forest, and before you drive along the valley of the great river, you will see Aedelwine standing there, still singing to the rising sun – as the Dragon Tree!

What became of the bodies of the savage Wyverns? The Dryads quickly covered them in moss, bracken, brambles and trees. You can still see the heaps today; they look just like random, rounded hills dotted along the valley floor. Now, people walk over them with their dogs and children play hide and seek amongst the trees, but no-one ever, ever tries to grow crops on these 'hills' or build houses on the slopes. It doesn't feel 'right' somehow, though nobody knows why – except you!

10 A MAP AND WHERE IT ALL BEGAN

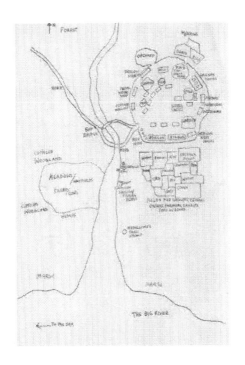

That looks like a dragon singing to the morning
sunshine…and that is where it all began.

ABOUT THE AUTHOR

Wendy Guilfoyle has lived in the Forest of Dean since 1984. It is a place of mystery, magic and wonder. She plans to write stories which bring some of that magic and mystery to all her readers.

Printed in Great Britain
by Amazon